SURRENDER

FIONA COLE

Copyright © 2020 by Fiona Cole

All rights reserved.

Cover Designer: Indie Girl Promotions

Interior Design: Indie Girl Promotions

No part of this book may be reproduced or transmitted in any form or by any means, electronic or mechanical, including photocopying, recording, or by any information storage and retrieval system without written permission of the author, except for the use of brief quotations in a book review.

This is a work of fiction. Names, characters, businesses, places, events and incidents are either the products of the author's imagination or used in a fictitious manner. Any resemblance to actual persons, living or dead, actual events, or locales is entirely coincidental.

*To everyone who loved Jake and Jackson.
Thank you.*

1
JAKE

"Mom, this dinner is delicious, as always," I complimented, the rich tomato sauce from the lasagna almost making me moan with each bite.

"I totally agree, Joanne. Your cooking is always a treat." Jackson took a bite and didn't hold back his moan. It wasn't meant to be sexual, but I couldn't hear that sound and not immediately think of all the ways I could make him do it again. "It's a shame you didn't pass your cooking skills on to Jake."

"Ha. Ha," I mocked.

He looked across the table and winked before taking another bite, making sure I was watching when he slicked his tongue across his lips. He was playing with fire and knew it. I couldn't wait to get him home and force him to his knees before filling his mouth, making him moan around my cock. And I knew he'd return the favor, making me love every second.

This man was my best friend—my fiancé. I looked at him and my heart tripped over itself, beating harder with all the love I had. Who knew how much things could change in a year? My lips tipped up slightly when I thought of all the changes he brought to my life.

Hell, this time last year, I was engaged to Carina. So sure of my future. So sure of who I was as a man—a straight man.

Until I saw Jackson again.

He'd flipped my world upside down without even trying, making me realize that was the way I was supposed to be the whole time. I loved him more than I thought possible and he held my hand through every step I fought to accepting myself.

"I told you, Jackson, call me Mom," my mom admonished.

"Yes, Mom."

"And where is that brother of yours?" she asked with a raised brow.

"He's on a date tonight. He was bummed to miss your food. I was sure he was about to cancel his date, but well...he's Andrew."

"Yes, ever since he began walking again, he's been very...active."

That was a polite way of putting it. Andrew had done a lot of physical therapy over the past year and got some mobility back in his legs, allowing him to use arm braces to walk. He said it was just enough of an injury to bring the ladies in.

"Yeah. Active," Jackson said dryly.

"Well, I'll be sure to send you home with some leftovers for him."

"Thank you, Joa—Mom."

We finished the rest of dinner with small talk about how our week had been. It was all normal and perfect.

But it was hard to focus on the conversation with Jackson constantly making innuendos and eye-fucking me across the table. The way he ate the breadstick almost had me demanding he follow me to the bathroom right fucking now.

My mom was oblivious as she sipped her wine and laughed at Jackson's stories about the bar he co-owned.

"I can't eat another bite." Jackson rubbed a hand down his firm chest and leaned back before patting his washboard stomach. He rubbed his hand back up his chest and held my stare with heated eyes. I wanted to jump up from the table and leave now, but I needed a moment to get my cock under control before I scarred my mom with the boner trying to burst through my zipper to get to Jackson.

I opened my mouth to make an excuse to get out of here, but my mom beat me to the punch.

"Now, time for dessert," she exclaimed, clapping her hands.

"Mom, I'd love to but—"

"I won't have it. I picked up some stuff especially for you," she said before walking through the doorway to the kitchen.

"Eager to get home, baby?" Jackson asked, a sly smirk on his full lips.

"Not really. Why?" I aimed for indifference, but the way I had to swallow the saliva building in my mouth gave away how close I was to drooling over him.

"I figured you'd be eager to get home so I can bend you over the couch and fuck that tight ass of yours."

I scoffed. I loved this game with him. "You can try. I'll have you pinned to the wall within two seconds of stepping through the door."

"That's fine. Perfect position for me to shove you to your knees and make you take my cock."

I couldn't help it, I groaned. My hand drifted between my legs and squeezed my throbbing length. Jackson watched the movement and it was his turn to swallow.

"God, I can't wait to be inside you," I said breathlessly. "Any way I can. Your ass or mouth. I just need you."

His fists clenched on the tabletop and I think we were both about to jump up and leave without saying goodbye. Hell, we'd probably have to stop halfway home just to relieve the intense ache.

"So, I happened to be at a bakery," my mom cut through the thick tension burning between us.

I took a handful of deep breaths before I could look up. She set a tray on the table, holding small rectangles of cake, all of them different.

"What is that?" I asked.

"Well, I went in for some cannolis, but we got to talking and I told her you were planning a wedding, and one thing led to another, and she sent me home with these."

It came out in a rush and I barely held back my sigh. Jackson and I had been engaged for a while now, but we hadn't done much wedding planning. Not that it stopped my mom. She was so eager to have "the most beautiful wedding ever" that she constantly looked into things. I couldn't blame her. She planned events all the time for charities and fundraisers, so planning parties was in her blood. Planning her son's wedding was the pinnacle, as she explained it.

I looked over to Jackson and the heat from his eyes dimmed. I caught his stare and he smiled, but it looked strained. Jackson tended to be close-mouthed about the wedding, and it bothered me, but I wasn't too concerned. Jackson and I loved each other and if big weddings didn't excite him, then that was fine. As long as I could call him my husband, that was all that mattered.

"Thank you, Mom. These look delicious."

She sighed in relief. "Oh, good. I know I'm supposed to wait for you boys, but I couldn't help myself. And what's the harm in a little extra cake?"

She sat down and began explaining all the flavors. There were about nine different cake combinations, all with different fillings and icing and they began to blur halfway through.

"She said you can call and schedule a better tasting. She sets up a whole display so you can create your own combinations. She's really amazing—one of the top bakers in the area. She was even on one of those baking competitions and won."

"She sounds expensive," Jackson muttered.

"Nonsense," my mom waved his comment away. "There's no such thing when it comes to planning your wedding. Speaking of, do we have a date yet?"

I looked over at Jackson, but he was staring down at his plate, mashing his fork into the leftover cake. I knew he was just as frustrated as I was about not having a date set. The only difference was that he was the one putting it off.

"Daniel hasn't been able to give dates that Jackson can take off yet. He's opening that new place in New York and will need Jackson to cover while he's away. So we're trying to plan around that."

"Well, that's awfully selfish."

"Mom."

"It's my son's wedding," she defended. "A mother wants to plan these things."

I laid my hand over hers. "I know and we appreciate it. We'll let you know as soon as we do."

She gave a small smile, turning her hand under mine and giving it a squeeze. "Thank you."

I looked to Jackson to find him watching our hands with something akin to guilt in his eyes, but I was sure I was reading him wrong. It was probably just nausea from all the cake we ate. "You ready to go?" I asked him.

He blinked out of his stare and met my gaze, nothing but love shining there. Maybe I'd imagined it all. "Yeah," he answered, standing to collect his plate.

"None of that," my mom stopped him. "I've kept you boys long enough. Head home and get some sleep. I've got clean up."

"Are you sure?"

"Of course."

"Okay. I've got that meeting tomorrow, so I appreciate being let off the hook," I said.

"Make sure you tell Carina I said hello."

"I will."

Even though Carina and I ended our engagement—in a brutal way—we still remained friends. She'd been my closest friend for most of my life. So, while it took her a while to not—rightfully—hate me, she did become my friend again. We'd never be as close as we once were, but she was extraordinarily important in both Jackson's and my lives. Hell, if it wasn't for her, I'd never have ended up with Jackson.

Mom walked us to the door, making sure we took the extra cake home, and stood on the stoop as we went to the car.

"Thanks again for dinner, Mom," Jackson said.

"Make sure you let me know which flavor is your favorite, okay?"

We both nodded and closed the doors. We hadn't even made it to the end of the long driveway before Jackson's hand was between my legs. "I want to know which flavor is your favorite when you eat it off my dick."

I pressed on the gas and broke a few traffic laws to get home to find out.

2

JACKSON

I covered the yawn threatening to unhinge my jaw before lifting the coffee to my lips.

Standing outside the Netherland Plaza, scanning the crowd for Jake, I wondered when the last time was that I hadn't yawned constantly. At least a month ago. Maybe two?

I'd been picking up extra shifts at Voy *and* Voyeur trying to save every penny. Between Andrew's physical therapy, his new medical equipment, and this wedding that grew larger by the second, I wasn't sure there were enough hours in the day to work to cover it all.

I was one flower bouquet away from starting to perform again at Voyeur just to make more money. Not that I would ever do that to Jake, but dammit, I was struggling to keep up. A year ago, he was set to get married to a successful woman who could've paid for her wedding ten times over, and now there was me—poor, struggling me.

Of course, I didn't mention it, because he'd call me crazy and say what was his was mine. He'd wave it off and say that if his mom was the reason the wedding got so big, then let her pay for it. But she wasn't my mom—not really. Mine had died years ago and hadn't left me with much. I didn't have a family member promising to pay half the wedding as they sent me off into holy matrimony.

Who came up with that shit anyway?

But mainly, I didn't mention it, because he always looked so happy when his mom talked wedding planning. He didn't care, but he loved giving his mother something to focus on and that made me happy. Happy wife, happy life.

A chuckle slipped past my lips when I imagined Jake's reaction if I called him my wife.

Never in my life did I imagine being here: engaged and planning a wedding to a man. I'd almost always known I was bisexual, but I never thought I'd find someone to be enough for me to settle down.

Until him.

I saw his face through the window of the hired car, but had the wind knocked out of me when he stepped out and gave me that perfect smile. I fought the urge to run to him and pull him in for a kiss right there on the busy street. I craved to feel the rough brush of his scruff against my mouth as he aggressively feasted from my lips.

His mom stepped up behind him and before I could greet her, he leaned in to press a quick peck to my lips. "Hey."

I swallowed at his nearness, trying to bring moisture back to my mouth. "Hey."

His rough fingers of one hand slipped between mine and the other moved to wrap around the hand holding the cup, forcing me to bring it to his lips. He didn't break eye contact as he took a sip and I wondered how the hell watching his lips wrap around the lid of my cup could make my dick jerk in my pants.

"Hello, Jackson," Joanne greeted, squashing any erection.

"Hello, Joa—Mom." I was still getting used to calling her

Mom. She loved me like a mom, and I cared for her deeply, so I had no issue with it. But I'd known her since Jake and I were in college and she'd always been Mrs. Wellington or Joanne.

She tugged me down so she could place a chaste kiss to my cheek. "I love hearing that."

"Anything to make you happy."

She gave me a loving smile, like any mom would. "Let's head inside. We're meeting Andre Dorne for a tour."

I'd only been inside the Netherland Plaza once when my parents attended a fundraiser and brought me along. I'd looked up in awe at all the dark woods, golds, and intricate designs. It'd been huge and overwhelming to twelve-year-old me. It was *still* overwhelming to me. Now, I looked at each antique design and all I saw was dollar signs. This place was expensive—not in a subtle way, but in a way that screamed.

Joanne greeted a thin man in a dark suit who held his nose in the air but also gave a genuine smile and firm handshake. The next hour passed in a blur of various rooms and the history behind each one that made it so unique and a top selection among couples. Joanne oohed and ahhed over it all. The bigger it was, the more excitement crept into her face.

Jake nodded and paid attention, keeping my hand clasped in his until I pulled away with the excuse to use the restroom. In reality, I needed to escape before he felt how sweaty each option made my hands. I splashed water on my face and took a few deep breaths. I looked as tired as I felt. The dark circles under my eyes made the brown even darker.

Shaking my head, I covered another yawn and left the safety of the restroom. Jake's laugh reached across the space and squeezed my heart, forcing it to beat harder and faster. It always did. I loved him. I loved him with every single cell in my body. Seeing his head thrown back with joy surrounded by the golds that matched his hair reminded me of that love. My own lips tipped in a smile and I knew then, I'd get married anywhere he wanted. I'd work triple shifts if it meant keeping him as happy as he looked now.

When I rejoined the group, Andre flipped open the binder he'd been carrying. "So, do we have a date in mind?"

All three sets of eyes turned to me and I stuttered over my tongue, tripping on words like I'd never heard of a calendar in my life. "Ummm...I—um...what month is it now?"

Joanne's hand slapped my chest playfully. "You're so funny, Jackson."

Breathing a laugh, I played it off, but couldn't ignore the way Jake's eyes narrowed at my reaction.

"We don't have a date set yet," he answered easily for me.

"Hmmm." Andre pulled down his glasses to the end of his nose and dragged his finger down the page. "We had a cancellation for five months from now in November. Just before Thanksgiving." He looked up and smiled like he was giving us the winning numbers for the lottery.

Joanne clapped her hands with excitement while I ran mine through my hair, scrambling for the right words.

"Oh, umm. So soon." I looked to Jake, who still had the questioning look on his face. "I'll have to talk to work."

"Make sure you do it soon because a cancellation will be taken quick. Usually, I'd go to our waiting list, but I love you both so much, I just need you to get married here." He was a little over the top, but the way Joanne agreed to every single extra package, I was sure he wanted that commission more than he actually cared about our marriage.

"Thank you so much, Andre," Joanne said. "We will definitely get back to you ASAP."

We all shook hands and made our exit. The hot, humid air of Cincinnati in June flooded my lungs, feeling better than the choking panic of that hotel.

"I'll leave you boys to talk. I'm going to go and have drinks with a friend. Make sure you keep me up to date on what you decide."

We'd made it about two steps away from the door when Jake finally asked the question I'd been dreading. "What's wrong?"

"Nothing's wrong," I answered, my shoulders slouched, my eyes glued to the pavement.

"C'mon, Jackson. Don't give me that bullshit answer."

"I just don't understand what the rush is."

"There's not a rush."

"Yet, here we are, and I can't even get a day off right now, and you want me to tell you when I can get a whole week off six months from now." The words found a crack in the stronghold I had them under and started flooding out. "I'm so damn busy. And you're going to be busy with Carina's maternity leave coming up. What do you want to do? Say fuck it and let everyone deal with the fallout?"

"It's not about being busy, Jackson. We've been engaged for six months and you won't talk about any of it."

"And you've been gay for all of a year. Things take time, Jake. I didn't rush you, so don't you dare rush me," I growled, stepping into his space.

I wanted to take the words back as soon as they slipped free. Watching his face crumple had my heart doing the same.

"Is that what this is about? Me not being gay enough for you?"

"No, tha—that's not what I meant." My hands dragged through my hair, tugging to relieve some of the tension.

"Are you putting it off because you think I'll run again? That I'll leave you?"

"No, of course not."

He stepped right into my chest, speaking so close the breath of his words hit my lips. "Because Jackson, I will drop to my knees right here and show the world how much I love your cock—how much I love you. I'm sorry for being scared before, but I've worked hard to show you how much I would shout from the rooftops that I'm yours."

I hated myself. He'd struggled with loving me—a man—when we first got together, but he'd claimed our love without fear now, and I never wanted to make him think I questioned it.

"I'm sorry it—I'm just sorry."

He didn't say anything, and I couldn't blame him. This had nothing to do with his sexuality. None of that mattered. We loved each other, and that was all either of us cared about.

I held his cheeks in my palms, forcing his blue eyes to meet mine. "I love you." Leaning in, I pressed a barely-there kiss to his lips. "I'm sorry I'm being difficult. I've just been working a lot, and I'm tired. It's no excuse."

He leaned in to press his own, firmer, kiss to my lips, and I accepted it with relief. "Let's have dinner tonight and get some drinks at Voy."

"Okay." I nodded and stole one more kiss. "I love you. More than anything."

"I love you too."

A band around my chest released at his words and I knew everything would be okay.

3

JAKE

Tucking the file of papers under my arm, I locked my office door. I hadn't planned to be in the office on a Saturday, but Jackson got a call that they were short at the bar before we could follow through on our dinner plans. We agreed to meet for drinks later and I figured I'd respond to some quick emails.

I'd almost made it to the elevator when a light from an open door down the hall caught my eye—an office I was very familiar with. I strode down and peeked inside. She was standing but looking down at some papers on her desk. She brushed an errant strand of hair behind her ear, but it just fell forward again. It was such a familiar move, I chuckled.

Her head jerked up and her blue eyes locked on mine. "Hey, Jake."

Her lips tipped up in an easy smile. A smile that spoke of years of friendship and not the heartbreak at the end of our engagement. I was lucky she forgave me because I wasn't sure what I'd do without her in my life. Other than Jackson, no one knew me better than Carina—the woman I was supposed to marry until I fell in love with Jackson.

"What are you doing here on a Saturday?"

She stood upright, her hand immediately going to the soft curve of her belly. "I could ask you the same thing."

"Jackson got called in and I figured I'd log a couple hours before meeting him for drinks." She nodded in understanding. We were set to run the company our fathers had created, and I was sure we had a lot more Saturdays ahead of us.

"I'm just finishing up. Got a few more emails to get to."

"Well, don't stay too late." I went to step out when I turned back. "Hey, you should come meet us later at the bar."

She made it a point to look down at her stomach and back up to me with an eyebrow cocked. "A pregnant woman walks into a bar. It sounds like the beginning of a bad joke."

I laughed because Carina could always make me laugh. When I should've walked away, I stayed and took her in. She was always beautiful, but the pregnancy really made her glow. Marrying her would have been a mistake for both of us, but I would always love her and because of that, I'd always worry about her. "Are you happy?"

She closed her eyes and sighed, a content smile slipping across her face. "Very."

"You're going to make a great mom."

"Thank you, Jake."

"And you've been quiet about who the father is, but I hope he knows how lucky he is."

She dropped her gaze back to the desk for a moment before smiling back up at me.

"I'll see you Monday, Carina. Don't stay too late."

And with that, I left my ex-fiancée behind to go join my current fiancé.

Jackson

Jake walked into the bar, and like a magnet, my eyes locked on him. It was easy with his blond hair and tall height. He caught my eye and smiled, stealing the breath right from my lungs.

He made his way through the crowd to where I sat at the bar already nursing a beer with my brother. A replacement came in not too long ago, letting me off the hook for the night.

"Hey, Andrew," he greeted without taking his eyes off me.

Before Andrew could acknowledge his greeting, Jake had already moved on to grip my face, pulling me in for a deep kiss. I couldn't stop the groan working its way up my chest. Every time he claimed me in public, my love for him grew. I knew how hard it'd been for him to come out as loving another man and pride swelled through me that he did it so openly—that he did it so openly for me.

"Yeah, baby. Get it on," my brother catcalled beside us.

"This isn't Voyeur, so I suggest you keep it PG," Daniel—the owner of Voyeur and the other co-owner of this bar—joked from where he sat on the other side of Andrew.

Jake lingered a moment longer before pulling away and doing the manly back slap with Daniel and sitting down with his own beer.

"How was your date, Andrew?" Jake asked across me.

"So good," he replied as he was winking at a girl across the bar. She ducked her head with a smile.

"So good you're already looking for another?" I asked.

Andrew slapped me on the back. "Too many fish in the sea, brother, to just settle for one."

I rolled my eyes while Daniel chuckled.

"How was the venue search today?" Andrew asked.

"Good. Gorgeous place. We're just taking our time and

looking around," I rushed to explain before Jake could bring up the whole date issue.

"So, will you be the bride all dressed in white?" Andrew asked, a smirk firmly in place. "Do you want me to give you away? I can lift your veil and kiss your cheek. Maybe even shed a tear at how much you've grown."

I gave him my best dead-panned stare and he just laughed.

A rough hand slid over mine, pulling my attention away and saving me from responding. Jake's lips moved right by my ear. "Dance with me."

I set my beer aside and let Jake lead me to the dance floor. He was a good dancer, but I was better. I learned how to dance dirty when I worked at Voyeur. Some people had stripper fantasies, and I was more than happy to act those out.

We moved to the beat, but when a slower Pearl Jam song came on, he gripped my hips and pulled me into him, lining our groins up perfectly. Sliding my hands around his neck, I dug my fingers into his hair and closed my eyes to the sensation of his growing erection rubbing against my own. At one point, he slipped his leg between mine just enough to rub against my aching balls and I almost came there on the dance floor.

By the end of the song, I was panting and desperate. I didn't say anything when I linked my fingers with his and dragged him behind me to the bathroom. As soon as I made sure it was clear, I locked the door and pushed Jake to his knees.

"Suck me. I want to come in that pretty mouth of yours."

"Maybe I don't want to." He looked up at me with a taunt in his eyes but didn't rush to stand as I undid my belt. "Maybe I want you to hold off a little longer until we get home."

"Shut up and put your mouth to work."

His eyes glazed over when I tugged my cock free and gave it a couple rough strokes right in front of his face. Fuck, I was so hard and if I didn't get in his mouth soon, I was going t—

My thoughts broke off on a groan when he licked the head, dipping his tongue between the slit. "God, yes."

I stumbled back against the bathroom counter and Jake grabbed my hips before diving down as far as he could go. The warm heat enveloped every inch as his tongue worked the underside. I buried my fingers in his hair and forced myself to look down and watch his lips stretch around my thick length.

"More," I barely breathed the demand. "I want your throat. All the way, baby."

He didn't hesitate, sucking me hard. When my skin pulled too tight and electricity shot down my spine, I gripped his head and fucked his mouth hard. He held on and let me do whatever I wanted.

"You want my cum?" I asked as I held him down on me, his lips pressed to the base. He looked up the best he could, his eyes watering from the head of my cock resting in his throat and managed a nod.

I pulled him off and he gasped, but I just jerked him back on and raced to the finish. If anyone was waiting outside the bathroom, they'd know exactly what was going on in here from how loud I moaned through my orgasm. I let go of Jake's head so I could grip the counter behind me to hold myself up. He took over, bobbing up and down and collecting every drop of my orgasm.

I stood there, gasping for air while he got to his feet and fastened my pants for me. Leaning in, he kissed me, letting me taste the salty tang of myself on his tongue.

"We need to leave now because as much as I want to bend you over this counter and fuck you. I need more time for all the things I'm going to do to you," he growled against my lips.

I didn't wait for any more direction. I unlocked the door and rushed out, pulling him with me, shoving bodies out of my way to reach the exit.

"Jackson," I heard Tony, my bartender, call from behind the bar before I reached the door. I took a deep breath so I didn't snap at him. You'd think a guy who just came as hard as I did would be less tense, but the promise of Jake's pleasure hung like a carrot in front of me and I hated to look away from it. "Where are those straws we just got in?"

My shoulders dropped, and I gave Jake an apologetic look. "This will just take a minute. I promise."

"I can get them," Daniel offered.

"No, they're behind some other shit. Not where they usually are. I'll grab them and then we're out of here."

"Be fast. I need inside you," Jake said against my neck before letting me go.

4
JAKE

I bit back my groan as I watched Jackson move back to the hallway we just came from. I should have bent him over the sink when I had the chance. Anything to release the aching desire hardening my cock to dangerous levels. I'd adjusted it to my waistband and untucked my shirt, but I was sure it could've busted through a cement wall.

I stepped up behind Andrew at the bar and finished off the beer he had sitting in front of him.

"Hey! Just because you were cock-blocked doesn't mean you get to steal my beer." When I didn't respond, he smirked. I braced myself because whenever a Fields man got that look on his face, something dirty was about to come out. On Jackson, I loved it. On Andrew, I held my breath and hoped for the best. "So, how was the bathroom?" he asked, his brows waggling as he brought his fist up to his mouth, imitating a blow job.

I couldn't help it, I laughed and the boner straining my pants began to fade.

"God, you're a pervert," Daniel said with his own laugh.

Andrew shrugged, unrepentant and drank from the new beer the cock-blocker—I mean bartender—sat in front of him.

Leaning to see past Andrew, I took the opportunity to talk to Daniel while Jackson wasn't there. "Hey, can I ask you for a favor?"

Daniel leaned both elbows on the bar, giving me his full attention. "Shoot."

"Can you cut Jackson some slack? You've been working him so damn hard and he's exhausted."

Daniel's blond brows shot up to meet his hairline, and I should have known then something wasn't right. But once I had an outlet for some of my frustrations, I needed to get it all out.

"We're trying to plan the wedding, and everything is on hold until you give Jackson a firm date on when you're opening the Voyeur in New York."

His brows dropped low and his lip curled. "What? Is that what he said?"

"Yeah."

Andrew's laugh started soft and slow but soon shifted to an all-out cackle. His head was thrown back and he even threw a few slaps to the bar for good measure. When he calmed down enough, he wiped a few tears from his eyes and faced me.

"Da fuck?" When I continued to stare at him like he'd lost his damn mind, he dropped a bomb I hadn't ever expected. "Daniel said he could take the whole year off to get married if he wanted to."

My chest crumpled in on itself. Slow at first, just a few cracks, but as the words sank in, it became an all-out gaping hole. Andrew laughed again like Jackson lying to me—making excuses to not marry me—was the biggest fucking joke he'd ever heard.

When he noticed my dead stare, he quickly stopped. "Oh. Yeah. Not funny."

"What the fuck?" I whispered to myself. How could he do this? Why was he doing this?

"Yeah," Daniel said slowly, probably noticing me pulling in on myself and just waiting for the explosion after. "He can have off whenever. He's been asking for all the extra shifts. Hell, I haven't seen him work this hard since he was struggling to pay for Andrew's medical bills. He's taking anything he can get."

"Anything?" Cold washed over my body. "Even at Voyeur?" The club where he performed sexual acts for strangers. Where he performed sexual acts *with* others. Was he letting other people touch him? Oh god, I was going to be sick.

"No. Not that," Daniel rushed to reassure me. "He wouldn't do that, Jake. He's just managing the floor and tending bar."

He didn't even like tending bar, so why was he asking to do it more often? Taking a deep breath, trying to take in oxygen so it could rush to my brain and help me think rationally for a minute, I thought about it. I thought about the last few months and tried to remember everything I'd missed.

Money.

My fist curled against the bar top and my jaw clenched. This was all about fucking money. Every time my mom brought up something, that look sparked in his eyes. The one I'd been ignoring and putting down to stress.

The more I thought about all the lies he'd been telling me, all the excuses to put off setting a date, my emotions spun round and round on the roulette wheel until they finally rested somewhere between frustration and anger and guilt for not noticing it sooner. But all of this could've been avoided if he'd just talked to me. We always promised to talk to each other—no holds barred.

Well, he was damn sure going to talk to me tonight, no matter what I had to do to get it out of him. We were setting a fucking date.

Jackson

I'd just pulled the straws out from where I'd kicked them in a corner when the storeroom door went flying open, clanging against the wall.

"What the fuck?" I stood, ready to yell at whoever thought it was a smart idea to slam doors in my fucking bar.

The words died in my throat when I saw Jake standing mostly cast in shadow in the dark hallway. His shoulders were pulled back and his fists clenched and unclenched by his side. My lips tipped up on one side, loving to see how eager he was to touch me. But when I scanned his body and finally reached his face, I realized it probably wasn't desire that had him holding back from reaching for me.

The muscle in his jaw ticked so hard I could see it under all the scruff. His nostrils flared under his eyes that raged like an ocean in an angry storm.

I dropped the box and rushed to him, hands out, worried about what put that look there. "Jake, what the hell? What happened?"

"We're going home, right now."

"What? Ja—"

"Right. Fucking. Now."

I froze, dropping my hands to my side, shocked at him almost yelling at me. Jake rarely raised his voice and never at me.

He snagged a hand around my bicep and dragged me past a guilty-looking Daniel.

What the hell was going on?

I tried to get him to stop, but he used sheer brute force to pull me all the way to the door, shoving people out of the way without apology. The cool night air hit me, and my mind was so lost trying to catch up to the change in mood, I stumbled behind him through the parking lot until we stood by his car.

"Jake?"

"Get in the car, Jackson. We'll talk when we get home."

"Can I at least know what the hell happened?"

He closed his eyes and seemed to be counting to ten. "Please."

Confusion had been the only emotion rolling through me since he came barging in. But hearing his pleading tone to not push him, the way he stayed silent the entire drive back home, fear washed over me like I'd never felt before.

I was going to lose him. I didn't know why, but I could feel it in my bones. I was going to lose him.

I should have married him when I had the chance.

5

JACKSON

The click of our front door felt like the preamble to our ending —like the last shot fired that would finish us off. I was so focused on all the reasons he was going to end it, that I was completely unprepared for the rough hand to my shoulder slamming me back against the door. I winced as my head knocked hard against the surface and opened my eyes to find Jake right in my face, his eyes alight with anger.

He could be mad at me all he wanted but hitting my head fucking hurt and lit a fire under my own frustration. I clenched my jaw to hold back my angry words, waiting for him to speak first. And when he did, all the breath was sucked from my lungs.

"Why won't you set a date?"

"What?" I played dumb. Maybe he didn't know.

"Why?" he shouted only a few inches from my face.

I couldn't handle lying directly to his face and the anger coloring his gaze was giving way to hurt. I hated seeing him hurt. "I told you," I muttered, dropping my gaze to the side. It wasn't a complete lie, more of an avoidance.

"Bullshit," he growled, shoving me again, pinning me in

place. My eyes snapped back to his, my anger upping with each aggressive push. "I just talked to Daniel about giving you time off for the wedding."

My mouth opened and closed like a fish out of water.

"Imagine how dumb I felt when he had no idea what I meant."

I was floundering, mad at myself for lying—embarrassed for the reasons I lied in the first place. Heat flooded my cheeks and it pissed me off. "If you didn't want to feel dumb, then you shouldn't have pried."

"You're right," he answered too calmly. "Because my fucking fiancé should have fucking told me."

I didn't know what to say. I didn't know what to do. So, I stood there mute, pinned to the door, clenching my jaw, waiting for him to just end it all.

Jake didn't appreciate my silence and stepped only inches from me, getting right in my face, not holding an ounce of his frustration back.

"So, why the fuck haven't you set a date? And try a little honesty this time." His condescending tone got under my skin because he knew exactly how much it would irritate me—he knew what got my anger up the quickest and when someone talked to me like a child, it hit all my buttons.

I shoved him back, trying to gain some ground in this losing battle. "Why don't you get out of my face?"

"Don't change the subject, Jackson."

Shoving my hand through my hair, I gripped the strands and tugged, needing the sting. "Jesus," I said with my own mocking tone. "You dragged me out of there like a child about to get spanked."

"That can be arranged."

Usually, I'd respond to that with a hell yes and fight to bend him over the couch and spank his ass as I fucked him. But this time, I knew it wasn't playful and I threw a glare in his direction.

He was breathing harder, his fists clenching and unclenching, and I knew I had seconds before he snapped. But I wasn't fast enough.

"Just fucking tell me," he roared.

I'd never heard him yell so loud in anger, but it wasn't the anger that did me in. It was the crack in his voice at the end that let me know how much I was hurting him.

My mind scrambled for a way out of admitting my reasonings, but the bottom line was that I'd rather be embarrassed than hurt this man any more.

I threw my hands out, raising my own voice. "Because I can't afford this wedding." I stomped over to him, the words flooding out now that the gates had opened. "I'm working my ass off to get any money I can to save." It was my turn to shove him, my eyes stinging. "For your fancy venue." Shove. "For your fancy cakes." Shove. "For your fancy flowers." One final shove, his butt hitting the back of the couch. "I can't fucking afford it."

Jake opened his mouth, but I wasn't done yet. I stepped against him, getting in his face now.

"And I'm not some kept woman, Jake. I'm not a fucking charity case."

"You think I give a shit about any of that?" he asked, his face screwed up.

"You're always so damn excited with your mom. I know how much you were wanting a big wedding with Carina—in a church —and I can't give that to you."

He bumped his chest to mine, pushing me back. "Jesus Christ, Jackson. I'd go to the courthouse right now and marry you. I don't give a shit about the wedding." His hands gripped each side of my face and for the first time since we got home, his eyes softened, easing the fear that had been compressing my chest. "I care about *you*. I want *you*. I love *you*."

A moan of relief rose from my chest and fell from my lips. It was the last of my argument—the last of the fear that he was dumping me. It was my white flag. He had me where he wanted me, and I loved him more than anything and I needed to remind myself that he was mine.

I fisted his shirt to hold him in place and attacked his mouth. The kiss was aggressive and hard and desperate. He gave back as good as he got, his tongue pressing through my lips to tangle with mine. His hands left my face and moved to undo my buckle. Yes, we needed to be naked, skin to skin. I ripped open his dress shirt and tore it from his shoulders, moving on to his pants next.

"Set a date," he murmured against my lips.

"What?"

"Do it. Give it to me." The words were slurred with pleading and desire, his lips barely leaving mine to give his demand.

My mind was slow, and I couldn't have told him what day it was today, let alone set a wedding date. Besides, the reasons for holding off were still there. "No."

He growled and bit at my lips, shoving my pants down my thighs before gripping my cock. He jerked me hard as we each pushed our pants off. When we were free of our clothes, he shoved me again, pushing me backward around the couch.

He was like a predator, stalking his prey. His eyes never left mine as he kept pushing, his fist on his own cock now. His eyes promising to make me scream in pleasure once he'd had his fill.

It pulled the caveman from me and urged me to fight for dominance. I let him move me where he wanted me because I wanted to be on that couch too. But when he asked me again to set a date, I still said no.

He shoved me again, the backs of my knees hitting the couch and forcing me to fall back. He quickly grabbed the lube from the end table drawer and fell to his knees between my spread thighs. My eyes fell closed as the warm heat of his mouth enveloped me.

"Fuck yes."

The snick of the lube opening was my only warning for what was coming next. Two blunt fingers swiped between my cheeks and I scooted down to give him better access. He didn't take time to tease me. He continued to suck on my cock like a fucking vacuum and pressed his fingers inside, swirling and spreading, getting me ready for his thick length.

I almost whimpered when he stopped sucking me.

"Set a date, Jackson."

"No."

My hips thrust when he nipped at the head of my dick softly. He took the moment to shove his fingers in hard, pulling a cry from my lips. I managed to pry my eyes open and look down my body to where he was swirling his tongue down to my balls. His other arm was flexing, and I knew he was jerking himself, coating himself with lube so he could fuck me.

"Fuck me. I'm done with the playing. Just fuck me," I demanded, knowing he wouldn't let me come until he was inside me.

He rose up and pulled his fingers from my ass with one last swipe against my prostate, only to press the head of his cock against my opening, but not pushing in.

"Set a date."

"No." But my refusal was weakening, and it escaped on a groan that morphed into a shout when he pushed all the way inside until his balls rested against my ass.

He started fucking me ruthlessly, his teeth bared like an animal rutting against his mate, making sure I knew who I belonged to. I reached down to stroke my dick, ready to come with him stretching me. But I only got two strokes in before he slapped my hand away.

I tried two more times with the same results and the last time I glared up at him. He gripped me at my base and squeezed, holding off my orgasm that was just beyond reach. Sweat coated my body. Breath sawed in and out of my lungs. My skin was tight, an electrical current running along the entire surface just waiting for one touch to set it off.

"Jake," I pleaded, reaching out to rub at his chest, pinch his nipple.

He fell over me, pressing his forehead to mine. "Set a date."

This time it wasn't a demand, it was a plea, said with a soft up and down stroke of my dick, promising to make me come harder than ever before. "God, fine," I caved. "We'll take the cancellation at the hotel."

The defeat was totally worth it when his full lips spread into the most beautiful smile. He pressed his lips to mine and jerked me perfectly, fucking me at just the right angle to make me come. I dug my heels into his ass and my fingers into his back, every muscle in my body flexing as my orgasm tore from me, shooting between us, coating both our abs. Another aftershock worked its way through me at seeing my cum slipping between the grooves of his stomach.

His eyes slid closed and he pressed inside me one-two-three more times before he held still and groaned his release into my neck. I held him through his orgasm, stroking his hair, kissing every inch I could reach with my mouth.

We stayed pressed together on the couch in the aftermath of our argument. The yelling from earlier now replaced with our heavy breaths.

I gripped his hair and jerked him back to look at me. "That wasn't fair."

But he was unrepentant with his lazy smile and glazed eyes. "When it comes to making you my husband, I will fight as dirty as necessary for you."

How could I argue with that?

I returned his smile with my own, bringing him down so I could taste his lips. "I love you."

"Love you too."

After a few more slow kisses between catching our breaths, he slid out of me and stood, offering a hand to help me up.

"Now come shower with me. I still need to feel your mouth on me tonight."

6

JAKE

A WARM MUSCULAR arm draped over my side, curling around to hold me close to a firm chest and hardened cock pressing against my ass. I stared down at Jackson's arm, so perfectly wrapped around me. His skin deliciously stretched over ropes of muscle that I could even see without him flexing. I loved the contrast of his bare arm against the colorful tattoos that covered mine.

Entwining my fingers with his, I lifted his hand and pressed it to my lips, smiling at the resulting groan behind me. He shifted as he woke, but I kept his palm in mine, not ready for him to roll away and stretch. I was rewarded for my stubbornness when he ground his cock between my ass and pressed soft kisses from my shoulder to my neck.

"Good morning," he said against my ear before nipping it. I loved the rough growl of his morning voice.

I rolled over and faced him, taking in his bleary eyes still adjusting to the light shining in through the blinds. They were so beautiful, the sun making them shine like melted chocolate, bringing out the tiny specks of green you'd never know were there unless you were inches from his face.

I loved him so much and I was going to make him mine if it was the last thing I did.

"Good morning."

He smiled and shifted closer, laying his head on my pillow. We laid there in silence for a while, just enjoying being close to each other, relishing the soft moment after last night's aggressive lovemaking.

Eventually, his brows dropped, and the ease of the moment slipped away. "I'm still worried about the money."

"I know, and I understand." I cupped his cheek and brushed my thumb along his sharp cheekbone. "You know it's our money, but I also know you're a prideful son of a bitch. More stubborn than I am."

My words brought the smile back, but it was brief.

"I just know how much your mom wants the big wedding."

"But you know I don't care, right?"

I held my breath, waiting for his answer. When he nodded, I exhaled hard and kissed him.

"I'm not going to lie, though," I said when I finally separated my lips from his. "It's going to be nice, standing in front of all those people, showing off my sexy, new husband."

One side of his mouth quirked up before he shifted and nipped at my thumb. "You going to prance me around?"

"Like the best show pony there ever was." We laughed, but I needed him to know how serious I was about the wedding not being a big deal to me. "You have to understand that this big hoopla is more for my mom than either of us. She's happy we're happy and wants to make a big deal about it."

"I know."

"Good."

Jackson rolled on top of me and pressed his thick length against mine, pulling a groan from my chest. He bit and licked at my lips before moving to my neck and back up again. Digging my hands in his hair, I held tight and thrust my hips.

"I love you," he growled against me, grinding harder, faster.

"I love you too."

More than he knew. With each second that passed, the ache in my balls grew, matching the ache in my chest. Looking up into his dark eyes staring down at me with more love than I ever thought possible, the need to make him mine grew and grew until it took up too much space in my chest.

"Jake," he groaned, keeping his eyes open as he came all over my stomach. The pleasure rippling across his body—the delicious friction against my cock had me falling right behind him.

He dropped his head to my shoulder, his hard pants heating my skin more than it already was. Despite coming, the pressure on my chest was still there, the need too big to contain.

"Marry me. Tonight."

His head jerked up. "What?"

"Let's go to Vegas and get married." The words tumbled from my mouth as they were forming in my brain, without thought. But my mind knew what it wanted, and it wanted this man as my husband. "You can buy the plane tickets. Pay for our real wedding. Mom will pay for the pony show."

His eyes were wide, but I could see the idea taking hold and how much he liked it. "Jake..."

"We'll still have our big day. We don't have to tell anyone. This is just for us." I brushed his cheek, needing to touch him. "Marry me."

Finally, the smile I knew and loved stretched his full lips and I knew everything would be perfect. "Okay."

An hour later, Jackson sat at our kitchen table in just his boxer briefs, dragging both hands through his hair. Frankly, I could have watched him all damn day in that position.

His arms flexing with every rough drag.

His abs rippling with each fidgeting move.

"There are no fucking flights for tonight. What the hell?"

I walked behind him and rested my palms on his broad shoulders, looking over the screen. "What about that one?"

"That's first class."

"So?"

"Do you know how much it costs to fly first class across the country?"

"Jackson, I—"

"Don't even offer," he growled.

Sliding my hands down his pecs and finally giving in to touch each ridged groove on his abdomen, I whispered in his ear, "Then buy the fucking flights." He hissed when I nipped his ear. "And I'll book the hotel."

"Dammit, Jake."

I cut his irritation off when I slid lower and gripped his soft cock through this underwear. "Do I have to punish you again." He thrust up into my hand, growing hard by the second. "Sometimes I think you're a stubborn ass because you like to bottom for me."

"Don't act like I don't own that ass as much as you own mine," he moaned, reaching behind me to grip my ass.

"You won't be getting this ass at all if you don't make an honest man out of me."

"Cocktease," he grumbled as he booked the tickets.

I smiled, giving him one last long stroke before heading to my own computer to book our hotel.

Just when I hit confirm, my phone rang.

"Hey, Mom."

Jackson plopped down on the couch next to me and I closed the laptop, not wanting to hear him bitch about the price of our room. It was our honeymoon after all.

"Hey, baby. I was just thinking of you, as always, and thought I'd call to check up on if you and Jackson had come to a decision about the venue."

"Wow, a whole twenty-four hours, Mom. I can't believe you waited this long to call and ask."

"Oh, hush. You know how excited I am. And this is an opportunity. If you pass on it, you may not be able to get married for another two years."

"The horror," I gasped.

"Don't make fun of your mother."

I laughed and Jackson pulled the phone out of my hand, putting it on speaker.

"Hey, Mom. We talked, and we decided to take the date."

Excited squeals made both of us wince and pull the phone away. "Oh, boys. You are going to have the best wedding ever. I promise. Just leave it up to me. I'm calling him back now."

"Mom, we can call—"

"Nope. I'll do it. I'm also booking a fitting for your suits. And flowers. Oh, and wine. Obviously, an open bar. We aren't heathens."

Jackson paled with each suggestion, but I gripped his thigh. When he turned wide eyes to mine, I merely leaned in and pecked his lips, offering him comfort without words, letting him know it would all be okay.

"We're definitely not, Mom," I said once I pulled away.

"Okay. Well, I'll let you two go. Enjoy your day. Leave it all up to me. Love you."

"Love you too," we both said.

As soon as I hung up, I gripped his cheeks and made him meet my eye. "Tomorrow you will be my husband. Nothing else matters. This is *our* wedding. And we're splitting it fifty-fifty."

"Okay. Yeah. I'm good."

"Good. Now let's go pack so I can fuck my husband."

7

JACKSON

"All right. Marriage license is booked. Same as the chapel," I said.

We'd just boarded a red-eye to Vegas and everything was coming together. I'd even splurged on the more extravagant package for the chapel. The one that came with a video. I wanted to remember this forever.

"Perfect."

I kissed my fiancé and settled into my overpriced airplane cubby. When the attendant came by, I gladly accepted the champagne.

Through the flight, I managed to find the balance between getting my money's worth out of this seat and not arriving in Vegas trashed. However, I was extra tired. Even in one of the cities that never sleeps, I couldn't wait to get to our hotel and rest my eyes for just a bit. Besides, I knew tonight would be a sleepless one filled with surrender.

"Don't even start," Jake reprimanded when a hired car pulled up outside the airport to take us to our hotel.

My side eye grew more intense with each floor we climbed at

the freaking Bellagio. All of a sudden, my first class tickets were mere pennies compared to the suite he booked us.

"You keep looking at me like that, and I'm going to fuck your throat harder than ever before."

"I'd like to see you try."

He smirked and my cock jerked behind my pants. God damn, I was always ready for this man. The thought of fighting him for dominance made the rush all the more intense, like sticking a fork in a socket.

Instead of starting the fight, he slapped my ass and stalked toward the bedroom, barely glancing at the beautiful view beyond the floor-to-ceiling windows. "Come curl up with me for a few hours before I make you mine."

We set an alarm and curled into each other's arms, Jake's head firmly planted on my chest, his strong thigh thrown over mine.

He woke before me and when I got up with the alarm, he strutted back into the room with his hands behind his back and a big-ass smile on his full lips.

"I went ahead and ordered our suits."

"What? Dammit. I'm paying for this one. I would have gotten us—"

He jerked two white T-shirts out from behind his back, still wrapped in plastic, a pseudo-suit screen-printed on the front.

I couldn't help it. I fell back on the bed, shaking with laughter.

"Are you fucking kidding me?" I asked, wiping tears from my eyes.

"As a heart attack. Got to have the full Vegas experience."

"I guess I should be grateful they're both suits and one isn't a wedding dress."

"That would be fun to explain in photos."

He tossed me my shirt and we got ready. I came out of the

SURRENDER

bathroom to find him bent over, tying his shoe. He stood tall and dragged his hand through his blond hair. For a moment, I couldn't speak. I couldn't breathe. I think my heart stopped just before it started hammering a beat that sounded a lot like mine.

We'd been through so much and he would be mine. Fucking finally. The man I never thought I'd have was going to be mine.

"You okay?"

It seemed too good to be real.

"Are you sure?" I asked, letting the doubt have a voice.

"More than anything. I love you."

"I love you too."

Another hired car waited for us at the entrance and instead of complaining, I gripped my fiancé's hand and kissed his cheek. "Thank you."

We rode in silence to the chapel and in no time at all, standing under the bright lights of Las Vegas with the cheesy Elvis impersonator looking down from his altar, I heard the most beautiful words of my life.

"I now pronounce you husband and husband. You may kiss your groom."

We kissed and kissed, all while Elvis sang.

As soon as it was over, we rushed back to our hotel, declining any offers of champagne and extra pictures.

We burst through the room, clutching each other, shoving, gripping, fighting for dominance.

In the end, I was the victor, shoving him against the glass of our suite, turning him to face the lights of the fountain below. Biting his neck, I pushed his hands to the glass and stripped us of our clothes.

"You want my cock, husband?"

"Fuck yes," he moaned.

"Not yet."

I dropped to my knees and spread his cheeks apart, flicking

my tongue along his tight hole. His breaths grew heavy and his pleas desperate. Especially when I reached around him to grip his shaft and stroked him roughly.

My own cock throbbed between my thighs and my need grew beyond control. Having lubed him with my tongue and stretched him with my fingers, I stood, holding his cheeks apart to spit on where I needed to be.

I held my hand to his mouth. "Lick."

He complied, sucking on my fingers before I could pull away. I used his saliva to stroke my cock and then lined my head up with his opening.

"I love you, Jake."

"I love you, Jackson—my husband. The love of my life."

With a groan of happiness and pleasure, I pushed in and fucked my husband in front of the entire strip.

I did what I'd wanted to do since I was a teenager.

I claimed him as mine and let him claim me as his.

I surrendered.

EPILOGUE

CARINA

"Hello, Laura. I'm here to see Erik."

I'd been visiting Bergamo and Brandt since earlier in the year as a little side project. They wanted to open an office in London and reached out to Wellington and Russo for assistance. Since we'd already helped them set up their current business almost eight years ago, they didn't need a whole team like they had before. No, they needed me and what I wanted to offer. So, without really discussing it with my father, I supplied them with a marketing plan completely created by yours truly. A damn good one, if I said so myself.

Jake helped out a few times when I needed to run numbers and analytics, but he didn't need to waste time away from other projects that needed his full attention. So, he signed when required, and we hadn't brought my father on.

"Look at you." Laura beamed, taking in my belly. "You're radiant, Carina."

"I'm sweating," I deadpanned, making her laugh. "Why the hell is it so hot in September?"

"Because you're pregnant. It's the law that all things to make you uncomfortable will happen in the last trimester."

I rolled my eyes but shared a laugh with the older woman. She'd had three kids of her own, so she was kind enough to listen to me whenever I came in.

"I'll let him know you're here," she said, picking up the phone. A moment later, she let me know to go on in.

I opened the door, and my eyes first locked on Erik rounding his desk. I saw others in my periphery in the seating area around a coffee table and remembered today would be a full team meeting.

"Hey, Carina. Can we get you anything to drink?" Erik asked, placing a gentle kiss on my cheek. We'd become close over the past few months of working together—friends. I'd also become close to his girlfriend, Alexandra, who gave a smile and a wave on her way to the couch. At least, as close as I let people get these days.

I opened my mouth to accept some water when a voice had me choking on my words.

"Carina?" A deep voice croaked my name, pulling my eyes to the others on the couch.

Dark hair pushed back, and the most startling gray eyes I'd never forget, even if I tried.

Holy shit.

"Ian?"

What were the odds? What were the *freaking* odds?

"You two know each other?"

My gaze jerked to the petite brunette sitting pressed to Ian's side. Hanna Brandt, Erik's little sister who worked in another department on the floor below. Her eyes were wide and scanned my body, resting on my stomach. It wasn't anything she hadn't seen before, but as she looked between Ian and me, probably connecting the dots, it took on a hint of worry I'd never seen before.

I looked back to Ian to find his eyes widening as they took me in. My hand rested possessively on my stomach like I could hide the giant belly from his accusing eyes. If he looked shocked before, it was nothing compared to his jaw-dropping gawk now.

"What the hell is that?"

Want more from Carina and Ian? Check out her book, Another—a surprise pregnancy romance.

You can read Jake, Jackson, and Carina's full story in Lovers. Free on Kindle Unlimited.

See where the Voyeur series all began in the forbidden, student-teacher romance, VOYEUR.

If you're looking for a little more angst in your books you can check out my new adult, second chance romance, SHAME. Find out how Anna and Kevin discover each other and learn to understand their unique sexuality.

Don't miss out on any of my upcoming books, giveaways, and important news by signing up for my newsletter... Fiona Cole Newsletter.

You can also join my Facebook reader group, Fiona Cole's Lovers, for exclusive sneak peeks and teasers.

ABOUT THE AUTHOR

Fiona Cole is a military wife and a stay at home mom with degrees in biology and chemistry. As much as she loved science, she decided to postpone her career to stay at home with her two little girls, and immersed herself in the world of books until finally deciding to write her own.

Fiona loves hearing from her readers, so be sure to follow her on social media.

Email: authorfionacole@gmail.com
Newsletter
Reader Group: Fiona Cole's Lovers

www.authorfionacole.com

ALSO BY FIONA COLE

The King's Bar Series

Where You Can Find Me

Deny Me

Imagine Me

Shame Me Not Series

Shame

Make It to the Altar (Shame Me Not 1.5)

The Voyeur Series

Voyeur

Lovers (Cards of Love)

Savior

Another

Watch With Me (Free Prequel)

Liar

Teacher (Pre-Order Now)

Printed in Great Britain
by Amazon